This Little Tiger book belongs to:

_____

_____

_____

To Sarah ~ A B

To my nephews, Arthur & Wilf ~ R W

LITTLE TIGER PRESS LTD,
an imprint of the Little Tiger Group
1 Coda Studios, 189 Munster Road,
London SW6 6AW
Imported into the EEA by Penguin Random House Ireland,
Morrison Chambers, 32 Nassau Street, Dublin D02 YH68
www.littletiger.co.uk

First published in Great Britain 2019
This edition published 2019

Text copyright © Anna Bowles 2019
Illustrations copyright © Richard Watson 2019
Anna Bowles and Richard Watson have asserted their
rights to be identified as the author and illustrator of this
work under the Copyright, Designs and Patents Act, 1988
A CIP catalogue record for this book is
available from the British Library

ISBN 978-1-78881-366-2
Printed in China • LTP/1400/4633/0522
8 10 9

FAIRYTALE CLASSICS

Pinocchio

Anna Bowles

Richard Watson

LITTLE TIGER
LONDON

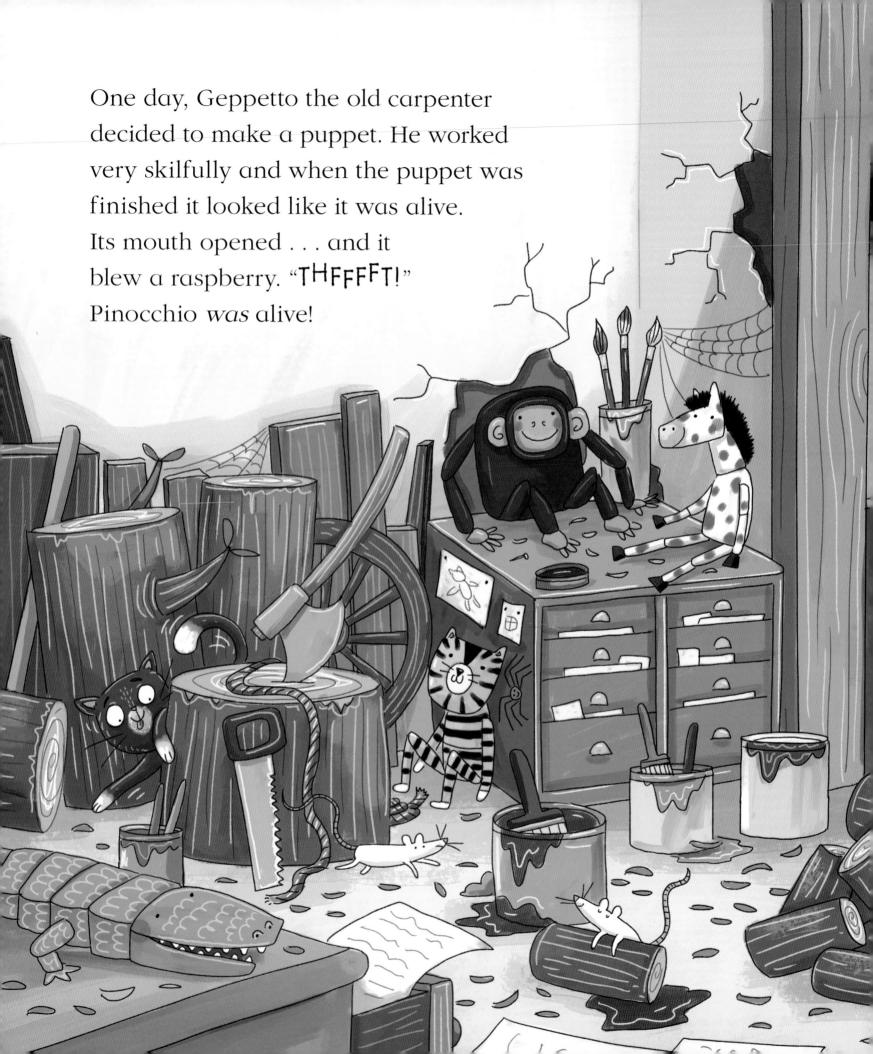

One day, Geppetto the old carpenter decided to make a puppet. He worked very skilfully and when the puppet was finished it looked like it was alive. Its mouth opened . . . and it blew a raspberry. "THFFFT!" Pinocchio *was* alive!

Pinocchio cried, "You look **boring**. I want to see the world!" The naughty puppet ran outside – SMACK! into a pair of legs.

"What's all this?" grumbled the policeman. "Is that man chasing you?"

"Yes! He's a robber," Pinocchio lied.

Then a very strange thing happened. Pinocchio's nose began to grow longer . . .

Meanwhile, Geppetto was dragged off to jail!

Pinocchio sat at home feeling very pleased with himself. Suddenly, he heard a little voice . . .

Crik, crik!

"I am the Talking Cricket!" it said. "I will give you some advice to help you become a real boy.

Be good and kind and always do what adults tell you . . ."

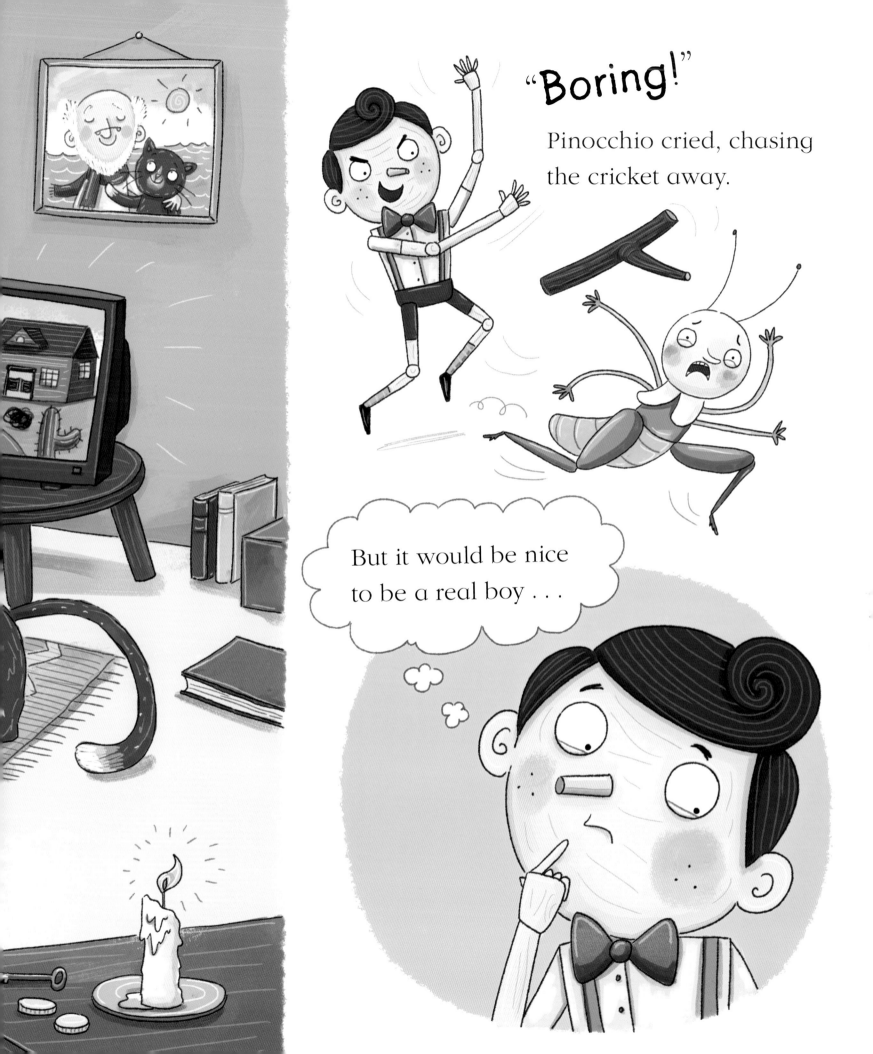

"Boring!"

Pinocchio cried, chasing the cricket away.

But it would be nice to be a real boy . . .

Kind old Geppetto forgave
Pinocchio for sending
him to jail.

"How do I become a real
boy?" Pinocchio asked.

"You will need to go to school," said Geppetto kindly.

"Oh," Pinocchio sighed.
That sounded no fun at all.

Boring!

"I'll go!" Pinocchio promised. But as he spoke his nose grew longer and **longer**...

Geppetto sold his coat so he could
buy Pinocchio a schoolbook.
Pinocchio was so grateful he
decided to go to school after all.

But on the way he saw a sign . . .

Pinocchio sold his book and bought a ticket.
"I've come to play!" he announced to the puppets.

They high-fived and
danced all day.

It was dark when Pinocchio left the theatre.

"Be careful!" warned the other puppets. But Pinocchio thought he was so clever he had nothing to be scared of.

Pinocchio was stopped by two horrible thieves.

Hello...

...little puppet.

"Don't hurt me. I haven't got any money!" Pinocchio said.

At last Pinocchio escaped. He ran until he reached a little house.

A kind fairy lived in the house.
She put Pinocchio to bed
where he tossed and turned.
"I'm ill!" he groaned.

The fairy brought him medicine.

"That looks horrible! I won't drink it!"

"Will!"

"Won't!"

"Will!"

"What if I don't?"

"You'll die."

Sometimes it is a good idea to do what adults say.

Sometimes . . .

When Pinocchio was better
he left the fairy's house.
He wanted to find something fun
to do, but instead he kept
thinking about home.

"I wonder what my father
is doing?" he said.
A pigeon heard him and landed on the road.

I've seen your father searching for you. He's terribly worried!

"I don't care!" Pinocchio snapped.

But to his amazement, his nose grew longer . . .

and longer . . . and longer!

He *did* care about Geppetto. Very much.

"I saw Geppetto rowing across the sea to look for you," said the pigeon.

"Can you tell him I'm here?" asked Pinocchio.

"Tell him yourself," the pigeon retorted, scooping Pinocchio onto his back and flying off.

"WaaaaAAAAARGH!"

When he'd got over his fright, Pinocchio peered down at the sea below. He saw . . .

a floating oar . . .

Geppetto's empty boat . . .

and a

HUGE SHARK!

"FATHER!" cried Pinocchio.

He wriggled so much that he fell off the pigeon.

Pinocchio tumbled **plop** into the ocean.

First he sank

down . . .

Then rocketed up . . .

Then tumbled **down . . .**
and was gobbled **up**
by the shark!

Eeek!

And what did he
see in the shark's
stomach?

Geppetto!

Pinocchio and his father hugged each other.

Pinocchio laughed.

"I'm made of wood! I can float you to shore."

They crept up the
shark's throat.
Pinocchio reached out
to tickle its nose . . .

ATISSHHHOOOO!!

They were free!

When they made it to the shore,
Pinocchio was too tired to walk.
Geppetto carried him home,
and they slept beside each other
all night.

When he woke up, Pinocchio cried,
"Father, are you all right?"
"Yes, my son," said Geppetto. "And look
what has happened to you."
While Pinocchio was asleep, he had
transformed. Smiling in the mirror he
saw a good, kind, amazing . . .

REAL boy!